FRANKLIN PARK PUBLIC LIBRARY

FRANKLIN PARK, IL.

Each borrower is held responsible for all library material drawn on his card and for fines accruing on the same. No material will be issued until such fine has been paid.

All injuries to library material beyond reasonable wear and all losses shall be made good to the satisfaction of the Librarian.

Replacement costs will be billed after 42 days overdue.

WHEN THE RAIN COMES

by ALMA FULLERTON

Illustrations by KIM LA FAVE

pajamapress

First published in the United States in 2017
First published in Canada in 2016

Text copyright © 2016 Alma Fullerton
Illustration copyright © 2016 Kim La Fave
This edition copyright © 2016 Pajama Press Inc.
This is a first edition.

10 9 8 7 6 5 4 3 2 1

www.pajamapress.ca   info@pajamapress.ca

The publisher gratefully acknowledges the support of the Canada Council for the Arts and the Ontario Arts Council for its publishing program. We acknowledge the financial support of the Government of Canada through the Canada Book Fund (CBF) for our publishing activities.

Library and Archives Canada Cataloguing in Publication

Fullerton, Alma, author
When the rain comes / by Alma Fullerton ; illustrations by
Kim La Fave.
ISBN 978-1-77278-012-3 (hardback)
I. LaFave, Kim, illustrator II. Title.
PS8611.U45W44 2016   jC813'.6   C2016-903702-9

Publisher Cataloging-in-Publication Data (U.S.)

Names: Fullerton, Alma, author. | LaFave, Kim, illustrator.
Title: When the rain comes / by Alma Fullerton ; illustrations by Kim La Fave.
Description: Toronto, Ontario Canada : Pajama Press, 2016. | Summary: "Malini, a young girl in a small Sri Lankan community, is anxious about the responsibility of helping with the monsoon-season rice planting for the first time. When a flash flood leaves her stranded alone with the ox cart full of rice seedlings, she summons unexpected courage to calm the ox and save her town's rice crop"— Provided by publisher.
Identifiers: ISBN 978-1-77278-012-3 (hardcover)
Subjects: LCSH: Sri Lanka – Juvenile fiction. | Rice -- Planting – Juvenile fiction. | Autonomy (Psychology) – Juvenile fiction. | Self-reliance – Juvenile fiction. | BISAC: JUVENILE FICTION / People & Places / Asia. | JUVENILE FICTION / Social Themes / Self-Esteem & Self-Reliance. | JUVENILE FICTION / Lifestyles / Farm & Ranch Life.
Classification: LCC PZ7.F855Whe | DDC [Fic] – dc23

Cover and book design—Rebecca Bender

Manufactured by Friesens
Printed in Canada

Pajama Press Inc.
181 Carlaw Ave. Suite 207 Toronto, Ontario Canada, M4M 2S1

Distributed in Canada by UTP Distribution
5201 Dufferin Street Toronto, Ontario Canada, M3H 5T8

Distributed in the U.S. by Ingram Publisher Services
1 Ingram Blvd. La Vergne, TN 37086, USA

FOR MAKAYLA, ANNABELLE, ARIA, ANIKA, AND CHLOE —A.F.

FOR MADDY —K.L.

MALINI lies in bed, waiting for the song of the bullock driver to rise over the chorus of spurfowls high in the trees.

She hears it distant and low,
coming closer as the sun wraps
its long arms around the mountains
in a good morning hug.

An ox's hooves join
in the morning
orchestra.

CLOP
CLOP

Malini rushes outside.
She watches
the load of rice seedlings
swish back and forth
on the cart as it bumps
over the road toward her.

Today she will learn
to plant those seedlings.

Over the next few months
they will grow strong
and bring food and fortune
to her village.
But what if

she does it wrong?

Will they still grow strong?

Malini swallows hard
biting on her bottom lip and
shifting her feet.

The bullock cart stops
beside her and the driver waves.
"Keep an eye on the ox," he says
before he ducks into the cafe
for a break after his long ride.

The ox snorts and shakes his head.
Malini backs away quickly.
He is big enough to crush her.

The wind picks up,
leaves on the trees

flip-flap

louder
    louder.

The skies go dark
and even the birds
take cover.

Their songs silenced
by wind whipping
through the palms,
bringing a sheet of rain
toward the village

POUNDING

POUNDING

POUNDING.

It comes closer,
and she wishes she could hide too,
but Malini must stay
with the ox.

Whoosh *whoosh* *whoosh*

BOOM

BOOM

BOOMING

against the tin roofs.

Her heart pounds
as loud as the rain

as it comes,

a waterfall

straight from the sky.

It carries the

CRACK

CRACK

CRACKING

of thunder
high over Malini's head

and a river of water,

swift enough to wash her away
rushes down her road,
blocking the bullock driver
from Malini and his cart.

Malini wants to run
inside her house to

safety

but the ox

MOO
MOO
MOOS.

He shuffles and shakes,
tied to his cart.
There is no escape for him
from the rice seedlings
sailing on the wind
across his back
like whips.

He stomps
at the water

rising

to their knees.

The driver is calling to her.

Her mother is calling to her.

Baba is calling,

"Malini, get to the barn!"

But Malini is

scared frozen.

The wind pushes against her.

It knocks her down.

She grabs the rein
to pull herself back up.

She must get the cart to **higher ground** or they will lose **all** of the rice seedlings meant for planting.

She
TUGS
TUGS
TUGS
on the rein
until the ox follows her
through the rising water

UP

UP

UP

the hill to Baba's barn.

Inside, she pulls the doors closed.

She unfastens the yoke
and sets the ox free
from the cart.

The barn shakes,
creaking.

Wind
howling.

She huddles against the wall,
thinking they might
blow away with the storm.

Rain seeps through
the leaky roof,
leaving puddles of water
on the floor.

The ox
bows his head
snorting
huffing
stomping.

She must steady him
or be crushed.

She leans close to him,
stroking
whispering
calming.

They wait
slowly,
breathing together

in

and
out
in
and
out.

They wait
until
the walls
no longer creak,

They wait
until
the pounding
on the roof
dribbles to a

TICK
   TICK
TICK,

and the river in the road
becomes an easy stream.

Malini swings open the barn doors,
letting the breeze

float

into the barn.

She leaves the cart
safe in the barn
and leads the ox

CLOP
CLOP
CLOP.

When she reaches home,

she is rushed
by a throng of hugs.

She lifts her face
        to the sky
            and listens

as the orchestra
of the spurfowls
rises again.